THE GRIMOIRE OF VALENTIUS THE WEREWOLF

THE GRIMOIRE OF VALENTIUS THE WEREWOLF
BY
ARUNDELL OVERMAN

Contents

INTRODUCTION

Hello, my name is Arundell Overman and I would like to present to you the Grimoire of Valentius the Werewolf. The following story may or may not be true. I love truth and almost never lie, and this story would have no meaning to me unless it were true. On the other hand, there is no such thing as werewolves and Skinwalkers, right? So, this story must surely be all made up. And maybe it is. I cannot say one way or the other, and you would not believe me if I did. Diablito is a nickname I was given once. I cannot be held responsible if you try any of the techniques in this book.

THE GRIMOIRE OF VALENTIUS THE WEREWOLF

Hello, my name is Diablito and I would like to introduce to you the Grimoire of Valentius the Werewolf. To explain what this book is, I must tell you that you have never read anything like this before, or ever will again. This small book is an instruction manual of werewolf magic given to me by the ghost of a werewolf named Valentius.

At this moment I am sitting at my computer, in a small apartment on the edge of Joplin Missouri. No one knows where I live or who I am really except one person in this city. I have erased my personal history as best I can and am prepared to start a new chapter in my life.

I am 45 years old, have brown hair and brown eyes and weigh about 150 pounds. My race is German and Native American of the Blackfoot tribe.

I realize that many of the things that I am about to say will be extremely hard to believe, even for witches. I have no choice but to carry on and explain the material as it was presented to me. First let me tell you how I came by this knowledge. I was raised in a strict Christian home. I was homeschooled, and I had little contact with the outside world beyond the family farm. I never accepted Christianity as a child and wanted to be a ninja. After that I wanted to be a rock star. I never had any paranormal experiences, and had no knowledge of the occult, but I was kind of dreamy.

At 16 a member of my parents' church began to talk to me about yoga, and I tried a little meditation. At 17 or 18 I had a spontaneous out of body experience, probably brought on by the meditation. I knew then that the spiritual world was real. I messed around with wicca for a year or so and began to read tarot cards. At 19 years old I met a demon named Asmoday. Like a genie from a lamp, he came out of a copy of the grimoire called the "Lesser Key of Solomon" and appeared to me, though I had never heard of his name, or even read that book yet. Asmoday has three heads. One is a man, another is a ram, and another a bull. He rides on a dragon.

After I met Asmoday, I was completely dedicated to magic and demons. I must have read 1000 books on the occult. I practiced thousands of rituals. I saw all kinds of spirits; I went out of body many more times. I joined a modern branch of the Golden Dawn and worked my way through all the grades. I even used the old Golden Dawn ritual for invisibility and went invisible in front of my ex-wife. Everything that I could possibly learn about magic, I learned it! Astrology, angels, demons, dragons, ghosts, crystals, yoga, tai chi, chi gong, ninjutsu, Satanism, Toltec, Kabballah, Taoism, grimoires, paganism, hypnotism, mind control, seances, anything and everything that related to the paranormal or the occult in any way, I wanted to know about it. Since Asmoday came out of the Lesser Key of Solomon, I must have read that book 100 times. I studied all the grimoires and their spells and practiced every form of ritual or mystical practice I could find.

THE WEREWOLF IN LORE AND LEGEND

One day a friend came over to my house with a book he proudly claimed to have stolen from our local library. It was called "The Werewolf in Lore and Legend" by Montague Summers. He said that he felt compelled to give the book to me and did not know why. I did not know anything about werewolves at the time, or that there were even any real books written on them. The book by Montague changed all that. He painstakingly detailed hundreds of cases of accused werewolves. I had no idea there were so many. Thousands of people were accused of being werewolves and put to death for it in the past. It was a phenomenon that roughly paralleled the witch burnings. In France alone between 1600 and 1700 there were 30,000 people accused of being werewolves. France had the most werewolf cases of all of Europe. Why?

One thing that I learned was that you did not become a werewolf by being bitten. No, that's only Hollywood. In the old days they believed that werewolves were witches who made a deal with the devil and then received a wolfskin belt or pelt that allowed them to transform. This was often in combination with a magic oil composed of a fat mixed with hallucinogenic herbs. There are many examples of this magic ointment in old witchcraft trials and it was called Sabbath ointment, Fairies ointment, Witches ointment, or Lycanthropic ointment. This ointment was believed to cause witches to fly.

Old spells show that the werewolf smeared the oil or paste upon their skin, put on the wolfskin belt, and then invoked the devil. That is how it was done. One can be sure that they would believe they had become a werewolf anyway once the drugs seeped into the blood stream. This in combination with the wolfskin belt and the invocation of the devil would tend to guide the persons state of consciousness toward that experience.

What happened to all these people? Were they simply mad, or tripping on the ointment? Yes, some of them. Some of them were also highly educated, the most brilliant minds of their age, musicians, witches, and alchemists. Eventually I was contacted by this crew. Maybe they had been around me my whole life, waiting for the right moment to teach me what they wanted to teach. It took me a long time to accept that these spirits do exist and decide to talk to them. My first memory in this life is of a werewolf in a dream.

I DREAM OF A WEREWOLF

Let me say that again. My first memory in this life is of a dream, and in that dream, there is a werewolf. I was perhaps three years old. I can remember nothing in this life before the dream. In the dream there is a small, square, black, stone pit down in the gravel driveway of the house I was born into. I found myself down in the pit. The night was clear and cool. Stars shone brightly far up above me in the sky. To my right was a werewolf. He was standing upright, wearing green pants, and a pink button up shirt with green suspenders. Hairy wolf feet extended from his pants, hairy, clawed hands from his shirt-sleeves, and his face was fully that of a wolf. His hair was blacker than the deepest black, and it moved slightly in the breeze.

I felt fear for perhaps the first time in my life. I did not know how I came to be in the pit, and I wanted to leave it. The wolf was chained to the wall of the pit with a heavy chain made of iron. I noticed that there were stone steps leading up out of the pit and I tried to take a step up the stairs. For some reason, my shoes were slippery and every time I tried to take a step my foot would slip. It seemed I was doomed to stay in the pit with the wolf. The wolfman did not seem to notice me and simply stared up into the night sky. Surely, he would see me at any moment and then I would be doomed... Time seemed to stretch on forever...

THE SPIRIT IN THE BOOK

My next encounter with the werewolf was after I started to read the book by Montague Summers. One day I noticed that there was something watching me read the book, I could feel it. I tried to tell myself that this was not so, and that there could simply be no such things as werewolves, but eventually I had to admit that something was watching me read. When you begin to study the supernatural, it begins to study you. I was simply drawn to the book like a magnet. I must have read it a dozen times.

Montague was not giving a manual of how to become a werewolf, no, most of the time he is recounting tales of what were probably crazed killers from another age, or the lurid, Satanic fantasies of witch hunters. Yet, beyond all the blood drenched stories, there was something else there, an intelligence, something not fully wolf or man, but perhaps in-between or both. I never saw this spirit as much more than a shadow moving out of the corner of my eye until much later. After reading the book by Montague on and off for years, one day I had an idea to create a spell based on the old werewolf spells and see if I could invoke some of the power of the werewolf myself. The basic idea was simple and went like this.

THE RITUAL OF WEREWOLFERY

On a Monday, which is the day of the Moon, the planet that rules the art of Werewolfery, or, on a Tuesday, which is the day of Mars, the planet which rules the wolf, at dawn, or dusk, draw or paint the magic square of Marchosias on the bare side of the skin of a wolf. Around this square add the sigil of Marchosias, and the signs of the Moon and Mars. Add to this your name, or a symbol of your name. Light some incense of Lavender, a scent of the Moon, or Dragons blood, for Mars, or both, and pass the wolf skin through the incense. If you cannot get a wolf skin, use a clean white linen to hold the spiritual power of the wolf, paint the magical symbols on the inside of it, and pass it through the

11

smoke. As you do so, say a prayer to the Lord of the Forest, the Devil, by whatever names you know him. Ask for success in your work, and for you to receive a wolf demon as a familiar spirit. Ask for strength, and for power, and for the wisdom to use the gift in the right ways. Use your own words. Then place the skin in a safe, and secret place. On the day of Mars, or of the Moon, purchase or create an oil that is safe for the skin and contains the scent of Mars or the Moon. When the oil is in your hands go immediately to a secret place and say the prayer to the Lord of the forest as before. Ask for success in your work, for strength, for power, and for the wisdom to use the gift in right ways. Then place the oil in the secret place, with the wolf skin.

When ready to use the skin take the oil and wolf skin from the secret place and say . . . *THERE ARE CERTAIN SORCERERS WHO, HAVING ANOINTED THEIR BODIES WITH AN OINTMENT WHICH THEY MADE BY THE INSTINCT OF THE DEVIL (put on the oil), AND PUTTING ON AN ENCHANTED GIRDLE (put on the girdle or belt), DO SEEM TO THEMSELVES AND OTHERS TO HAVE BECOME WOLVES, IN APPEARANCE, IN STRENGTH, AND IN POWER, AS LONG AS THEY SHALL WEAR THE SKIN.* (That is the moment of transformation, guard against loss of self, a type of mystical ecstasy often overtakes the soul) Spend some time in the skin, at least five minutes, take note of any sensations or magical knowledge gained from the transformation. Keep the mind still, empty, yet fully aware. You may also lie down and practice astral projection, projecting the form of the wolf out into the Astral plane. When you have returned, from the Astral projection, or your task or meditation is complete, take off the wolf skin. Stomp the feet or take on one of the physical body movements called magical passes of the Toltecs. * Flex the muscles of the body into the magical pass for a few moments and breathe deeply. Return to normal.

*See Carlos Castaneda "Magical Passes"

Note: For similar examples of the magic square presented here see "The Sacred Magic of Abramelin the Mage." This spell and the teachings of the Al Ghoul system of magic can be found in my book "The Al Ghoul Compendium, or The Black Book of the Grey Man." The sigil of Marchosias can be found in the Lesser Key of Solomon. The image of Marchosias shown in this book is from the 1863 Dictionnaire Infernal. The description of the demon following its image is from the Lesser Key of Solomon.

(35.) MARCHOSIAS. —The Thirty-fifth Spirit is Marchosias. He is a Great and Mighty Marquis, appearing at first in the Form of a Wolf having Gryphon's Wings, and a Serpent's Tail, and Vomiting Fire out of his mouth. But after a time, at the command of the Exorcist he putteth on the Shape of a Man. And he is a

strong fighter. He was of the Order of Dominations. He gover-
neth 30 Legions of Spirits. He told his Chief, who was Solomon,
that after 1,200 years he had hopes to return unto the Seventh
Throne. And his Seal is this, to be made and worn as a Lamen,
etc.

I HEAR THE MUSIC

Occasionally I would practice this ritual as a part of my regular magical practice. I had a few small things happen because of it such as I dreamed of a small grey wolf that wanted to play with me. I also had an experience that there was a werewolf spirit that briefly stepped into my body. There is a sensation of a wolf being under the skin. These experiences were mild compared to what was to come.

During the writing of my ninth book, "The Werewolf in Theory in Practice" I went much deeper into the study of the werewolf. I found pictures of the judges who sentenced the accused were-wolves to death and read trial transcripts. I studied what I could find of the Navaho native American Indian Skinwalker, a parallel phenomenon to the werewolf. Around that time, I began to practice the ritual of werewolfery I had devised more fre-quently. An energy began to build up around me that was thick, and hot and red. The sensation of transformation and the wolf under the skin began to get stronger and stronger. I started to hear music, a strange haunting song. I am a guitar player, so I would pick up my guitar and try to make the sounds I was hear-ing. It was exceedingly difficult, and I struggled with the piece for several months.

THE CASTLE

One day as I was playing the musical piece on guitar, I had a strange feeling come over me. It was as if I was transported to another dimension, a daydream so strong that It seemed real. In the distance there was a small castle surrounded by a moat. Weeping willow trees hung low over the water and the scene was both tranquil and imbued with an incredible power, like a cemetery. I began to write a story based around the scene. Like the song itself, it was not from inside my head, but rather something that I could hear and see.

I placed myself as a character in the story, that I was a young man who was going to learn to be a werewolf, and that there was a master werewolf that lived in that castle. I needed a name for the master werewolf, and one sprang to my mind powerfully, it was Valentius. I don't know where I got the name, I had never heard it anywhere, and thought I had just made it up. As it turns out, Valentius is a real name and means strong and healthy. I wrote a short story that included Valentius and the castle and placed it in the back of my book on Werewolves just for fun.

I decided that I would try to make a diary to record my experiences and really began to practice seriously, without telling anyone, remember that the first rule of werewolf club is, you don't talk about werewolf club. You really should never tell anyone that you are a werewolf, or would like to become one, or experiment with this magic. Total silence is best, people will not understand what you are doing and why. They will only think that you are crazy at best, or might try to eat them at worst, neither of which are true. Becoming a Skinwalker is about gaining control over yourself, not losing it.

So, for a couple months I recorded what happened to me as I would practice taking on the wolf skin. My wolfskin was made from an old blue tapestry with a pagan looking Celtic knot on it. There was so much energy around me because of my work I was high from it all the time. The diary gave a very sharp focus to my work. I felt an indescribable power flowing inside me. I grew physically stronger and started to see wolf spirits more and more. I was also doing a lot of yoga and body movement practices during that time and making offerings to the spirits. When I would play the song on guitar, I would feel the spirits gather around me to listen. I don't know where the song came from, but I know that it calls the spirits. I also started keeping close track of the cycles of the moon and spent a lot of time out in the moonlight watching it.

THE PAINTED LADY

One day I was out on the porch of the place I was staying, just looking up at the sky, and I had a vision. Once again, I heard the music, this time as if an orchestra were playing it. It felt like I was drawn forward, yet stayed in the same place, or as if a veil is pulled away and I am in another place. I am in a garden. It is evening time. There are large trees that provide a canopy above me and flower beds all around with flowers of various colors. In front of me about 6 feet away is a most beautiful woman dressed in the clothes of a 16th century royal. She had on an elegant black dress and it had purple and red flowers sewn into it. Her hair was piled high up on her head in the style of the day and she had a low-cut dress with her breasts barely covered at the nipples. One leg extended from her dress in a provocative way. I had a moment to take all of this in and grasp what I was seeing.

She was attractive, yet there was something very much like a whore about her. As if she was daring me to look at her and desire her. And as I looked her in the eye, I saw that her eyes did not look human, no, they looked more like that of a dog was my first thought, with exceptionally large pupils. I heard people laughing in the distance and thought that this must be a party or social gathering. A little girl ran by dressed in a white lacy dress. I looked at the woman and despite myself found myself lusting after her. She looked at me and said something that horrified me. "Why shouldn't we eat the little ones?" At that moment she raised her chin slightly and upon her pale neck there started to grow hair, thick like a man's beard. I knew what she was, a werewolf, and I could feel what she felt, the taste of blood upon my lips was intoxicating like a drug. It was all around me, a red, hot, thick energy. Yet I was horrified at the same time. I could not imagine eating children! My shock caused me to separate from the dream world and the vision vanished away. Yet it haunts me. Her makeup was so thick that she almost looked like a clown by today's standards, I am sure it was the style of the time. I call her the painted lady. Valentia. She scares me.

VALENTIUS

I ended up moving out of that house and into the apartment where I now live soon after that. I decided to scrap the old diary and start over. To get inspired and find direction, I burned some incense in a brass bowl as an offering to the wolf demon Marchosias and then sat down to write. Shadows began to move in the room.

"Just call me Valentius," the voice said. "I am the werewolf in your story, the master, the teacher, I am here to help you." I typed furiously as I heard these words, feeling encouraged. "I am outside of you so I can see things you can't" He continued. "This werewolf business is easy for me, I can step in and out of your body at any time, I can show you how to do all kinds of things, if you just listen to me." I felt afraid, here I was talking to the ghost of a werewolf. "What are you afraid of?" He asks.

I went down the list of my fears about my life. I said I was afraid about getting all my books finished and in print and finding the right editors. I said I was worried about getting a job to supplement my income as an author and dealing with the thousand trivialities of a workplace environment. I said that I felt like a hermit because I had spent the past 14 months writing books all day and I wanted to go out and find a new girlfriend and have a life for once. As if to reassure me Valentius then tells me that he was the werewolf in my dream as a kid, and that he has been with me my whole life. He said that he was the spirit watching me read the book by Montague, that he brought me the book to get all of this started.

Then he said that he was the one who gave me the song that calls werewolves. "You know I did, you know you didn't know how to do that stuff on guitar, the change from a minor key to a major key and back again is a technique that the classical masters used. I taught it to you." I feel the hair stand up on my arms as I write this. It was true. The song was hauntingly beautiful, and it was not something that I could have written. Then, the shadow behind me moved to stand beside me and I saw him, in the same manner as I saw the painted lady, as if I were pulled into another dimension. He looked to be about 30 years of age, and he had on an olive colored jacket and long curly brown hair. He had sideburns like men wore in the 16th century, an odd detail, which no man today would wear, they made him very wolfish looking. He had double canine teeth on each side which gave him a fearsome appearance. His eyes also, were bestial, with large pupils. Like the painted lady.

He told me a lot of things about my life in rather harsh terms, taking the time to criticize me as lazy and weak. He said that if I would only listen to him, he would make me stronger, and into something that I could not yet understand, but I would want very badly if I could. He emphasized that I needed to trust him, even though this would be difficult for me to do, as I would have to enter a scary world of werewolves. He then said that he had a magical, Alchemical formula that he wanted to teach me through a series of talismans. I was to get a notebook and try to draw them.

THE TALISMANS

So, I did. It took about three days to get the talismans fully formed. I would draw a circle and stare at the paper and ask him what was to be drawn. At that point I would hear a direct statement such as "The devil helps those who help themselves" and I would write it down. Or I would see a flash of light within the circle that I had drawn on the paper and then a geometric symbol such as a triangle or a square that was to be the main form of the talisman. For three days I worked on them. I received the basic form the first night, corrections on the second night, and then the final form on the third. This whole process was exhausting as I could think of nothing else, and it took tremendous amounts of mental energy. Finally, I rested and was done with the creation of the talismans.

Over the course of the past two weeks I have meditated on the talismans and their meanings and I feel that soon I will undertake the work described upon them with all of my will, and I know not what will happen. Valentius has explained to me that the system he is teaching me is a form of Alchemy and thus I must treat it like a science. The only way to understand it is to experience it, and to record the results in a diary like a scientific journal. This is the diary of a Skinwalker.

Before I begin the diary of science, I feel that I must lay down the basic principles of the formula given to me by Valentius and the culmination of my work up until this point. So now I will show you the talismans and describe what I know about them so far, though I am sure that my understanding will grow as I carry out the process described. There are 5 talismans, I will describe them in order.

1. This talisman has a triangle in the center upon which is written on the sides, TEMPORARY CELIBACY, DIET CONTROL, and CONTROL ADDICTIONS. In the center of the triangle is a circle with a dot in the center. The dot represents the individual consciousness, within the universe the larger circle, and placed there it shows the individual passing through the triangle like a door. The three symbols of Alchemy are placed around the edges of the triangle to show that it is a work of Alchemy. Salt, the body is connected to diet control, mercury, the mind, temporary celibacy, and the "mercury" of semen. Sulphur is the soul, and the control of the addiction. These are the three conditions of the grimoires, the things a magician must do to prepare for summoning demons and casting spells. This work summons demons, and it casts a spell. Once the conditions are fulfilled, in three days' time, the spell begins, the demon is summoned. This is called the "first door" because it opens a gateway between this world and the next world by purifying the

magician and preparing them for action. Three days beyond this "door" the witch has gathered enough energy to begin the work. Thus, it is written on the outer ring of the talisman "The spell begins three days beyond this door."

This is a process of alchemy fire because when these things are done, the body begins to heat up. The sperm has heat within it, the belly and the digestive force also has heat within it, and the diet control affects this. Also, to stop any addiction the willpower must be powerfully engaged, this is the fire of the will. So together, these three fires burn and purify the toxins out of the witch to prepare them for the action of the other talismans.

This is symbolized by a man meditating inside an alchemical vessel as a dragon breathes fire into it. Heat and power swirl within the energy field of the witch. It may often manifest as anger during this stage of the work.

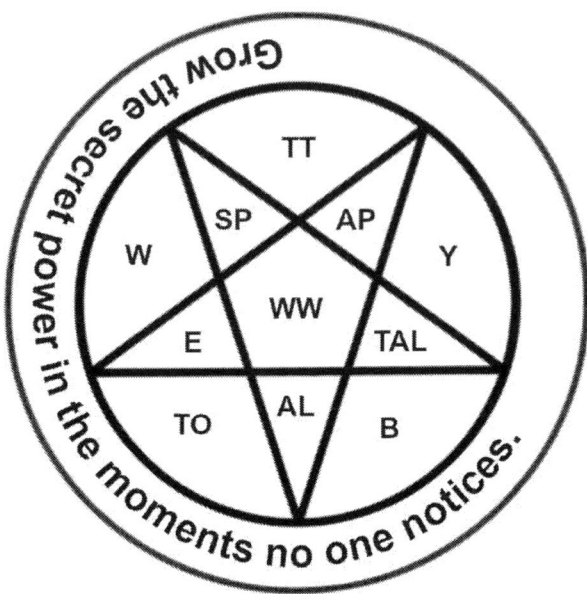

2. The second Talisman represents the work done in secret. This is several kinds of work. Primarily it is the work of magic. By that I mean invocations of spirits, casting of spells etc. It also relates to the body movements of yoga, or Toltec disciplines. To be a Skinwalker or a werewolf, you had to be the best of the best at witchcraft. My system of magic is the AG, so naturally, I have fit it within the symbol of an upturned pentagram.

This pentagram represents the head of the goat, and the devil, and all types of magic that fall under that category. One might practice from any number of grimoires and invoke any different number of demons or kinds of spells. The important thing is that you have a system of magic that has a means of invoking spirits, leaving the body, and casting spells, and also that it incorporates the body movement and breath control given in yoga practice, or that of the Toltecs, or both.

I will give you the basic meaning of the symbols but bear in mind that only if you research these systems and learn their magic will you be able to understand this power. Reading about it is nothing. The breath control and the postures change you!

Only when you can truly cast spells and you have practiced them over and over will you really be a master. It takes years to really understand these things. My hope is that one who comes after me will be even greater than I. And even after all I have learned, the final work is yet before me. I must live through the talismans and record this in a diary of science to see the full effect. But even now I have seen much!

Remember that the first rule of werewolf club is that you don't talk about werewolf club. It is the same for witchcraft. Don't tell anyone that you are a witch. The greatest resistance in our lives often comes from those people around us who are our family and friends. Listen carefully. The key to this stage is that you can withdraw to some secret place daily and practice your work. You must be able to perform the body movements and breath controls of the Yoga and Toltec systems, or you will never even come close to unlocking the true power. It can be a great challenge to find the time to practice. Thus, you must learn to "grow the secret power in the moments no one notices." This is no easy thing!

Learning this magic is not easy. You will have to spend many hundreds of hours reading and practicing. Everything will be easier if you simply do it when no one notices. Sometimes you may have to only do 5 minutes of yoga at a time. Or you may have to keep your wolf skin in some old, abandoned house and go there to practice the ritual. You can practice astral projection without any special tools, lying in your bed at night before sleep. You can whisper the words of an invocation to a spirit as you light incense, and no one will know. There are a thousand ways to do this. Who knows if you are taking a hot or a cold shower? You can generate power, in a way that no one notices.

The techniques are your keys, your tools. The magical passes, the spells, the invocations of spirits. These are all a part of your magic, and each has a specific place and purpose.

Here I list the basic forms and schools of my system of witchcraft. You can learn all of this in my book the Al Ghoul Compendium, or you may read the suggested books and train yourself in these systems. I read a thousand books on magic, perhaps you only might need to read 10 if they are the right ones. But you must read, and study, and practice with all your strength. When you understand all of this, you can try the magic of the werewolf if you want to. But if you can't do all of this, or something similar, don't waste your time, you won't get the full effect, and you won't experience the real power of the system of Valentius the Werewolf. Here is the description of the 11 parts of the second talisman, along with the letters which form their symbols.

1. Taoist Tantra. The Taoists of China developed an incredible magical tradition. I was introduced to this path through the works of Mantak Chia. I recommend you find the book "Taoist Secrets of Love: Cultivating male sexual energy." Read it and practice every technique. If you are a woman, there is a female version of the book. TT

2. Yoga. Yoga is a vast science. Here I recommend the Kundalini yoga taught by yogi Bhajan. This can be studied from the book "The Kundalini Yoga Experience: Bringing body, mind, and spirit together" by Darryl O'Keefe and Dharam Singh Khalsa. Read this book like your life depends on it and practice every technique. You will experience a flexibility of body such as you have never known and see the heart of the ancient tradition of Yoga. When you are ready, you may also study the 8 limbs of yoga as described by the sage Patanjali. Y

3. Breath control. For this I recommend a small book called "Ninja Power of the mind" by Toshitora Yamashiro. The breath and hand mudras given in this book awaken subtle powers. B

4. Toltec body movement. The Toltec system of magic was taught by Carlos Castaneda starting in the late 1960s. Carlos wrote many books which present the heart of Native American Shamanism in the modern age. His book "Magical Passes" reveals a system of body movement like Yoga, or Chi Gong. They awaken subtle energies, still the restless mind, and fill your body with a primal energy known as Tendon Energy. They are magical. TO

5. Witchcraft. In this instance I am speaking of the witchcraft of direct invocation of my gods, Asmoday and his bride the younger Lilith. This is usually done after the exercises of the previous four groups and consists of an invocation to my gods, and the offering of incense or Whiskey. In the Al Ghoul system of magic, there is a short cycle of techniques where the witch performs a small group of Taoist, Yoga, Breath control, and Toltec body movements. This warms the body up and rejuvenates it in marvelous ways. This is then directly followed by the invocation of one's own personal gods, and the offering of some small thing to them. W

6. Alchemy cold baths. In the Al Ghoul system, the witch is instructed to pull sunlight in tiny beams through the eyes, and to take cold showers or baths, and to meditate and purify the mind of restless thoughts through a method called recapitulation. For understanding of the power of the cold bath, see Wim Hof, an American Master of this peculiar power. AL

7. Astral Projection. The complete witch should practice the art of Astral Projection, the "out of body experience." For basic techniques on this I recommend "The Llewellyn Practical Guide to Astral Projection: The out of Body Experience" by Melita Denning and Osborne Phillips. Read it and practice it constantly until you develop skills in this area. AP

8. Evocation of demons and pagan spirits. For the evocation of demons, you must read "The Lesser Key of Solomon: The Goe-

tia" "The Grand Grimoire" "The Grimorium Verum" "The Grimoire of Honorius" and "The Sacred Magic of Abramelin the Mage." Those books are essential to understanding the demons of the western tradition and being able to conjure one of them. I built every tool in the Lesser Key of Solomon and worked it in the traditional manner for 20 years. I must have read it 100 times. Demons will come out of that book if you are meant to see them. E

9. The familiar spirit. Once you have contacted the spirits of the grimoires you will get a spirit guide, or several. This can come from a variety of places, but usually comes from one of the larger spirits assigning you one of its lesser demons to work with you. Usually some kind of talisman or link to the familiar spirit is created. TAL

10. Spells of all kinds. The grimoires previously mentioned also contain spells. You will have to research them and try them out until you have success and become a witch. Practice makes perfect. SP

11. The werewolf spell itself with the wolf skin. The werewolf spell is given earlier in this text. I also recommend that you read the book by Montague Summers, "The Werewolf in Lore and Legend" as well as my own "The Werewolf in Theory and Practice" to gain a full understanding of the legends of Werewolves and Skinwalkers. WW

The whole of this talisman is symbolized as a man within an Alchemical vessel with a dragon flying in a circle around him. Fierce winds are created by the dragon's wings. The form appears like the Ouroboros, the snake eating its own tail and refers to the dragon power, the kundalini. The dragon which breathed fire in the previous talisman has now entered the vessel and it has become sealed.

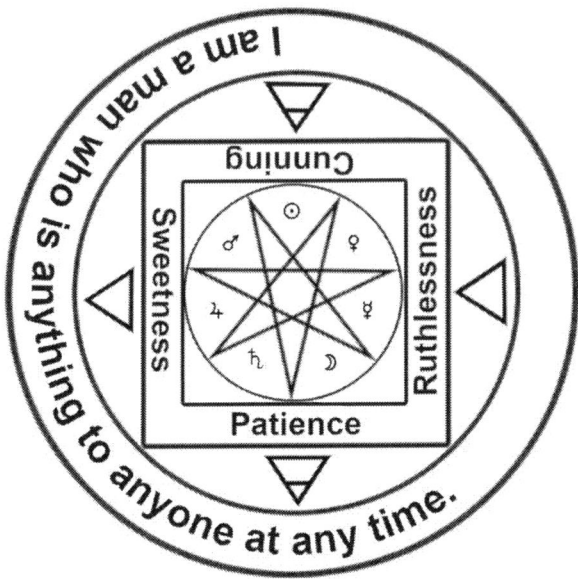

3. The third talisman is the work done in the world. In that sense it is the opposite of the second talisman, which is the work done in secret. This talisman can be described as a way of acting within the world. It can be called tactics, or strategy, or even lesser black magic and compared to stage magic. It is a square to represent stability and the material plane. The four moods are written on the edges of the square, and the four elements of earth fire, air, and water are placed at the edges of this. The 7-point star and the 7 planets are within a circle inside the square. This star represents the 7 principals of stalking as well as the 7 chakras and colors of the rainbow. This shows that the witch can act within all elements, and planetary alignments, and earthly conditions and chakras, and moods. They are whatever they need to be at any time, at any place, to anyone. Thus "I am a man who is anything to anyone at any time" is written around the edge of this talisman. The key to this talisman is a hunting strategy devised by the Toltec. It is called

stalking and has 7 principals.

The DEFINITION of stalking is this. UNBENDING INTENT toward a total goal. It can be defined as the art of GETTING YOUR WAY. It is a form of STRATEGY. When this form of strategy is applied to an ANIMAL, it produces the removal of a threat, or a meal. When this is applied to a HUMAN BEING, it produces the DE-STRUCTION OF AN ENEMY, the TRAINING OF A DISCIPLE, or a SEXUAL RELATIONSHIP. When it is applied to an inorganic being, a spirit, it produces an ALLY, a helper on the other side. When it is applied to THE SELF it produces a STATE OF TOTAL AWARE-NESS of the energetic body, the double.

The principles of stalking can be applied to all areas of life, such as human relationships, business clients or customers, etc. This is the art of sorcery, working within the physical world. The same principles, applied in dreaming, create the dreams of sor-cerers, which are not ordinary dreams.

There are 7 principles of stalking: 1. WARRIORS CHOOSE THE BATTLEFEILD. 2. DISCARD EVERYTHING UNNECESSESARY. 3. BE READY TO DIE. GO ALL IN. 4. ABANDON YOURSELF. FEAR NOTH-ING. 5. WHEN FACED WITH OVERWHELMING ODDS, RETREAT FOR A TIME. 6. WARRIORS COMPRESS TIME, EVERY SECOND COUNTS. 7. A STALKER NEVER PUSHES THEMSELVES TO THE FRONT.

This is symbolized as a man within a vessel standing upon a globe holding his hands up above his head within a half-circle lined with stars and planetary and zodiacal symbols. The half cir-cle stretches up above the globe and the man holds his hands as if reaching for or supporting the sky. Bolts of lightning radiate downward from the area above his head and pass around him toward the earth. This shows the man or woman pulling down cosmic rays and forces from the invisible realms in the ether and bringing them into the material plane, the earth. These vibrations look like sound waves or waves of water within the globe.

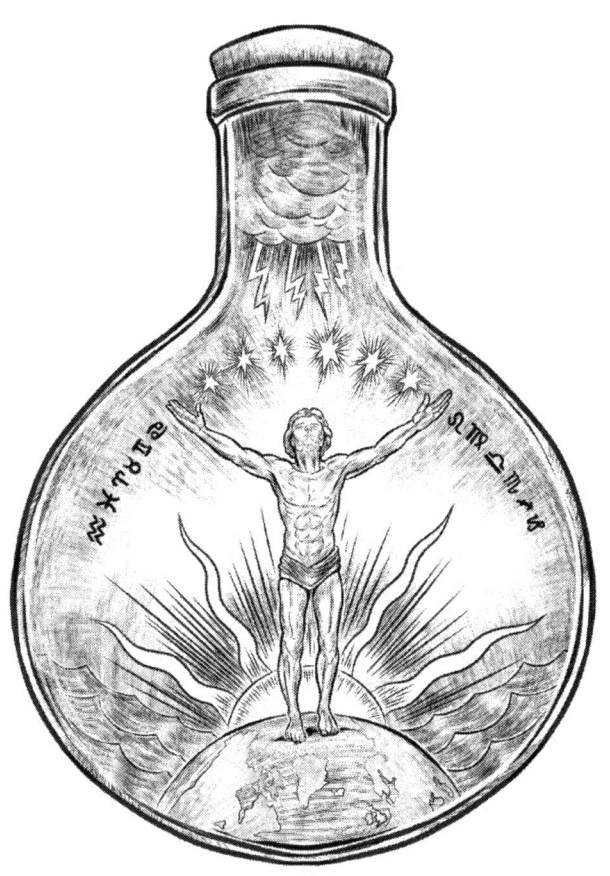

These formulas can only be understood through their application in the world and through practice. What I am teaching here is the most advanced magic I have learned throughout my entire lifetime. Spirits speak to us in the ways we understand. This magic has been designed for my own personal practice, but you can modify it in your own way if you choose to attempt it. You should have studied all the books I mentioned and will then see the universal formulas presented here and be able to modify them for your own needs. The magic will only be understood or accomplished by the most advanced witches. I am cutting you no breaks, I will not, and cannot make it easy for you. This will all be just talk unless you practice it as if your life depends on it. An interesting story. None of this is real anyway right?

If you become a master, you must teach one disciple. This is the rule in any art. Valentius made me. I wrote the book and gave it away to you. If you open its door, give the book away to one worthy student if possible, along with your best words of advice. Valentius is a werewolf of science, of alchemy, music, art, and medicine. He is an extraordinarily complex spirit, wise and full of knowledge. You will be like him in the end if you follow this path.

4. The fourth Talisman is composed of a downward pointing triangle within a circle. On the three bars of the triangle are written money, sex, and power. These are symbolized by a dollar sign a heart and a moon. The moon shows that power comes from magic in general, as the moon is a general symbol of witchcraft, but it also relates to the specific power of the werewolf as being governed by the moon cycle, and strongest when the moon is full or when it is completely black.

The fourth Talisman is the culmination of the others in that it takes place in secret and in the open though it is not always seen or understood. People will not necessarily understand that they are seeing a werewolf. They may understand it on subconscious levels or even conscious levels depending on their level of awareness. The spirit of the wolf will be present in your actions and in what you accomplish if the other talismans and stages have been mastered, there should be a demon that comes from the fourth talisman to hunt and seek the accomplishment of the three sides of the triangle within this talisman. We are predators, we may not need to be predators of evil upon the helpless, but we must seek to hunt these things, or we will never get them. "The devil helps those who helps themselves." There is a time for compassion and a time to have none. Only bring the most dangerous aspects of the wolf out when necessary. I am not teaching you this magic to be a terror unto your neighbors. You should see miracles in all three areas, or you are missing a step.

The fourth talisman is symbolized as a man with the head of a wolf and 6 arms. He may have the caduceus of Hermes extending from his groin, and female breasts, in the manner of the Baphomet of Levi. In the hands of the figure are held an incense burner as an offering before the gods, a sharp weapon representing destruction and protection, and alchemical vessel with the elixir of long life within it, a rose representing sexual pleasure, a bottle of whisky as an intoxicant representing altered states of consciousness, and a book containing magic spells and the history of the werewolf. Above this figure is a series of moons to represent the moon cycle, and he sits on a cubical stone made of earth. All of this is within the vessel of Alchemy. The whole figure represents both a stage of the work as well as a god or goddess which is both a reflection of the witch themselves, as well as a very real demon, an aspect of Baphomet, the devil. This demon will come forth because of the work and may be offered incense or Whiskey as an offering. It will communicate with the witch and do acts of magic according to its powers in return for offerings and sacrifices before its image.

5. The fifth talisman is the union of opposites and any talisman with a figure of 6 sides, a hexagram, would do. It is the final door, and when passed through it, you become what you were before. It is the simplest of the talismans and the easiest, because passing through that door requires only that you push upon it with your mind and stop working with the power of the other talismans. "Beyond this door you are what you were before." Simply be a mortal man again.

The action of this talisman is symbolized by a phoenix within the vessel of alchemy. As the phoenix is reborn from the ashes, so is the soul reborn in a new form. This completes the cycle begun by the burning fire within the first talisman.

I went through the first door and then fell. Over the course of the next few days, the process was within the symbolism expressed in the alchemical vessels was shown to me by Valentius.

I was not much of a student of Alchemy up until this time, and I am impressed with his formulas. I would note that for those who can understand, the 5 talismans relate generally to the 5 elements and to the formula of "Solve et coagula." I would like to draw them out or hire an artist to create them based off my drawings. He has given me another song as well during this time as well. It is hauntingly beautiful. *Note, the alchemical illustrations in this book were drawn by Ville Vuorinen and are not present in some early editions.

FINAL NOTES:

Stay hungry. Stay horny. Stay sober most of the time, enough so that the slightest intoxicant is great pleasure. To carry out the art of stalking takes practice, no matter what kind of animal you are, and only one who strives becomes a master, yet the talismans, the formulas themselves have a tendency to produce mastery over time, and the end result is long life and wisdom. A werewolf is not immortal. But the power rightly used can produce a life of great length and quality of experience. Beyond this I can tell you no more for I must undertake the work myself. This will be written in the Diary of a Skinwalker.

Since I have now explained my journey up until this point, it is time to begin the diary of the work. In this diary I will attempt to carry out the formulas described by Valentius the werewolf and record the results. So, currently I begin to push upon the first door. Here I go.

1 PM Sunday October 11th, 2020

Approved. -V

Blank pages provided for notes:

Printed in Dunstable, United Kingdom